D E A T H

the

high

cost

of

living

CONTENTS

4

introduction by
TORI AMOS

8

chapter one
THE SPIRIT OF THE STAIRWAY

38

chapter two
A NIGHT TO REMEMBER

66

chapter three
THE HIGH COST OF LIVING

95

DEATH TALKS ABOUT LIFE

102

A BRIEF HISTORY OF DEATH

104

biographies

WRITTEN BY
NEIL GAIMAN

ILLUSTRATED BY
CHRIS BACHALO
MARK BUCKINGHAM
DAVE McKEAN

COLORED BY
STEVE OLIFF/OLYOPTICS

LETTERED BY
TODD KLEIN

INTRODUCED BY
TORI AMOS

DEATH CREATED BY NEIL GAIMAN AND MIKE DRINGENBERG

T O R I

A M

S O

It's funny but on good days I don't think of her so much.

In fact never. I never just say hi when the sun is on my tongue and my belly's all warm. On bad days I talk to Death constantly, not about suicide because honestly that's not dramatic enough. Most of us love the stage and suicide is definitely your last performance and being addicted to the stage, suicide was never an option - plus people get to look you over and stare at your fatty bits and you can't cross your legs to give that flattering thigh angle and that's depressing.   So we talk.

She says things no one else seems to come up with, like let's have a hotdog and then it's like nothing's impossible. She told me once there is a part of her in everyon though Neil believes I'm more Delirium than Tori, ar Death taught me to accept that, you know, wear you butterflies with pride. And when I do accept that, know Death is somewhere inside of me. She was th kind of girl all the girls wanted to be, I believ because of her acceptance of "what is." She keep reminding me there is change in the "what is" b change cannot be made till you accept the "what is

Like yesterday, all the

recording machines

were

b r

µ ç

g u

d o

w n

again.

We almost lost a master take and the band leaves tomorrow and we can't do anymore music till we resolve this. We're in the middle of nowhere in the desert and my being wants to go crawl under a cactus and wish it away. Instead, I dyed my hair and she visited me and I started to accept the mess I'm in. I know that mess spelled backwards is ssem and I felt much better armed with that information. Over the last few hours I've allowed myself to feel defeated, and just like she said if you allow yourself to feel the way you really feel, maybe you won't be afraid of that feeling anymore.

When you're on your knees you're closer to the ground. Things seem nearer somehow.

If all I can say is I'm not in this swamp, I'm not in this swamp then there is not a rope in front of me and there is not an alligator behind me and there is not a girl sitting at the edge eating a hot dog and if I believe that, then dying would be the only answer because then Death couldn't come and say Peachy to me anymore and after all she has a brother who believes in hope.

t o r i   a m o s

(Tori Amos has been playing the piano since she was 2 years old. She was accepted into the Peabody Conservatory at the age of 5. She was kicked out for irreconcilable differences at the age of 11.

At 13 she was playing bars in Georgetown, Washington D.C. chaperoned by her father, a Methodist Minister. She continued playing in bars 5-6 nights a week for 11 years, until the release of "Y Kant Tori Read," recorded on Atlantic Records.

Back playing bars after "Y Kant Tori Read" met a quick death. Realizing the piano was "her thing," Tori started writing again at the piano. The songs written during this period became the basis for "little Earthquakes."

Tori moved to London, playing clubs alone at her piano. "Me and a Gun," an EP containing "Me and a Gun and "Silent All These Years" was released in October, 1991 in the UK and caused quite a stir.

"Little Earthquakes" was initially released in the UK in January, 1992 and worldwide release followed. A 1992 world tour gave Tori a chance to eat lots of good food! She played over 200 cities worldwide alone at her piano.

Currently, she is happy that recording is almost finished with her new project. The album is due for release in early 1994 and will be supported by a world tour of her and her piano.)

DEATH: THE HIGH COST OF LIVING

Published by DC Comics. Cover, introduction and compilation copyright © 1994 DC Comics. All Rights Reserved.

Originally published in single magazine form as DEATH: THE HIGH COST OF LIVING 1-3 and DEATH TALKS ABOUT LIFE. Copyright © 1993 DC Comics. All Rights Reserved. Vertigo and all characters, their distinctive likenesses and related indicia featured in this publication are trademarks of DC Comics. The stories, characters, and incidents featured in this publication are entirely fictional. DC Comics does not read or accept unsolicited submissions of ideas, stories or artwork.
DC Comics, 1700 Broadway, New York, NY 10019
A division of Warner Bros. - An AOL Time Warner Company
Printed in Canada. Sixth Printing.
ISBN: 1-56389-133-6

Cover and publication design by Dave McKean

T H E

S P I R I T

O F

T H E

S T A I R W A Y

My name is Sexton Furnival, but I'm pretty much used to it by now, and this is the last thing I'm ever going to write.

This is because there's no point to anything, and I've thought about this hard and long.

Okay. I figure, I'm mature. I know my own mind. I'm sixteen —almost sixteen and a half. And what have I got to show for it?

For a start I don't have anybody I'm in love with.

To be honest, I think love is complete bullshit. I don't think anyone ever loves anyone. I think the best people ever get is horny; horny and scared, so when they find someone who makes them horny, and they get too scared of the world outside,they stay together and they call it love.

Second, I don't have anyone I hate

I mean, I know a hell of a lot of assholes. But that's all they are. Assholes.

There's no one I know who's evil. I mean, in books and movies you get the bad guy, and you know immediately who the bad guy is because, well, he's bad. And you've got the good guy and it doesn't matter what he goes through, he knows who the bad guy is.

And I don't even have a faithful sidekick.

Well, you may not think this stuff is very interesting, or a reason to end it all, or anything, but you're wrong.

Well, maybe not wrong about it not being interesting, but you're wrong about it not being a good reason for checking out early.

I mean, there's no point to anything.

And if there's no point, you might as well be dead.

It's not as if anybody's going to give two shits.

ok, Sylvia, when you ad this, I'm really not ying that you've been bad mother. But I'm t saying that you've en a particularly od one.

Let's leave it at that.

d, look, don't blame it on Steve either. He's been much of a her. I mean, he's still asshole, but I expect t just goes with being awyer.

st time I saw him he d me this joke.
hat's the ference between a uyer and a herring?"
don't know, Dad."
ne's wet and slimy d it stinks--and the er one's a herring!"

No, I didn't laugh either.

teve is actually pretty imy. I mean, he's a ollywood showbiz wyer, and he's got a rlfriend who's about y age, and he's rich nd, actually, now I ome to think of it, my ther is the best argu- ent against material uccess I know. nother good reason to rget about living.

Sylvia always tells me that she put him through law school. He was going to be the hippie lawyer...

I suppose I should give thanks for small mercies.

I read somewhere that suicide notes are a cry for help. Well, not this one.

This one's a statement of belief. Or of disbelief. Because there's nothing in the way of adult bull-shit I do believe.

Which is another thing I'm different from my mom on, because she believes in everything. I mean, it changes every week, but I figure by now she must have believed in everything.

SEXTON? EVERYTHING OKAY?

HI, MOM. SHOULDN'T YOU BE AT THE RESTAURANT TODAY?

NOPE. I GAVE MYSELF A DAY OFF. WE MADE MARLON PERMANENT CHEF YESTERDAY, SO I FIGURED IT'D BE GOOD TO STAY OUT OF THE *WAY* FOR A DAY.

WHAT'RE YOU DOING?

HOMEWORK.

YOU *WANT* ANYTHING? A *COKE* OR ANYTHING?

NOPE.

That's the other thing. I don't <u>want</u> anything.

So I might as <u>well</u> be dead. Right?

YOU REALLY OUGHT TO TALK TO THEM. EVERYBODY KNOWS THAT PLANTS LIKE TO BE TALKED TO.

SYLVIA, WHAT PLANTS LIKE IS WATER.

WHEN I WAS A KID YOU'D BUY PLANTS EVERY MONTH. THREE WEEKS LATER I'D WALK AROUND, EVERYTHING WOULD BE BROWN AND DEAD AND I'D GO ROUND AND THROW EVERYTHING OUT. THEN THE NEXT WEEK YOU'D BUY NEW PLANTS AND START AGAIN.

I'M SURE IT WASN'T LIKE THAT, DARLING. PLANTS ARE OUR LITTLE GREEN SISTERS.

SYLVIA, I EVEN USED TO HAVE TO WATER YOUR STUPID DOPE PLANTS, FOR CHRISSAKES.

I'VE BEEN THINKING. DON'T YOU THINK IT'S TIME FOR A REALLY GOOD SPRING CLEANING?

IT'S THE MIDDLE OF JULY, SYLVIA.

SPRING CLEANING. I MEAN, JUST LOOK AT THIS APARTMENT. IT STINKS.

OH NO.

I THINK MAYBE YOU SHOULD GO OUT FOR THE REST OF THE AFTERNOON.

I'M IN EARTH MOTHER MODE. THESE LITTLE FINGERS ITCH TO CREATE. LIKE THE MOLE AT THE BEGINNING OF WIND IN THE WILLOWS.

HOLD ON. I GOTTA SAVE THIS FIRST.

HI BILLY.

HHHNNN.

NO, SHE'S HOUSE-CLEANING. I'M OUTTA HERE. I'LL BE BACK LATE TONIGHT, I SUPPOSE.

HHHNNN.

I'M SORRY, IS BILLY BOTHERING YOU?

NO, MRS. LING. IT'S FINE.

I TELL HIM NOT TO SIT OUT HERE IN THE CORRIDOR. IT'S JUST HE GETS BORED SOMETIMES.

YEAH, I KNOW HOW HE FEELS. SEEYA, MRS. LING. BYE, BILLY.

HNN. HHHNN.

SO WHAT WERE YOU DOING ON THE *GARBAGE DUMP*, THEN?

BREATHING.

BREATHING?

UH-HUH. BREATHING. YOU?

I WAS THINKING.

ANYTHING IN PARTICULAR?

JUST THAT I DON'T WANT TO LIVE IN THE SAME WORLD AS THE *WORLD WRESTLING FEDERATION* AND THE *HOME SHOPPING NETWORK*.

CUTE. DOWN THIS WAY.

HI, MRS. ROBBINS. C'N I TAKE A COUPLE OF APPLES?

SEXTON.

WHAT?

SEXTON.

NOTHING WRONG WITH THAT NAME. HOW LONG YOU KNOWN DIDI?

YOU *THINK* I'M IN THIS BUSINESS FOR MY *HEALTH*, HUH?

YEAH. GO ON. HEY, DIDI--THERE'S A *PACKAGE* FOR YOU OUT BACK. I *SIGNED* FOR IT. YOU WANT TO GO *GET* IT?

IT'S ON THE TABLE.

YOU GOT A *NAME*, BOY? I'M AMELIA ROBBINS, BUT YOU CAN CALL ME MRS. ROBBINS.

TEN MINUTES. SHE FOUND ME IN A GARBAGE HEAP.

APPLES 79¢ lb

ORAN 89¢

WELL, YOU BE *GOOD* TO HER. SHE'S BEEN THROUGH A *LOT* LATELY. HER WHOLE FAMILY'S PASSED AWAY LAST MONTH. SHE DIDN'T *TELL* YOU ABOUT THAT?

SOME GUY WENT UP ONTO THE SIDEWALK, PLOUGHED INTO THE CROWD. KILLED DIDI'S MOM AND HER POP AND HER LITTLE SISTER AND SOME GUY SELLING CHEAP WRISTWATCHES FROM A SUITCASE.

GOT IT!

SHE'S STILL *LIVING* UP THERE BUT--

INSO GROCERY

BANANA 59¢ lb

APPLES 79¢ lb

ORANGES 89¢ lb

18

UH-HUH. YOU KNOW, HAS IT OCCURRED TO YOU THAT MAYBE YOUR FAMILY GETTING KILLED, WELL, STUFF LIKE THAT CAN *DO* STUFF TO PEOPLE...?

HAVE YOU THOUGHT ABOUT GETTING *HELP?* I MEAN, SEEING A DOCTOR, OR A PRIEST, OR SOMEONE?

I THINK *REALLY* YOU SHOULD *SEE* SOMEONE.

OH...

OH, *THAT'S* NO PROBLEM, SEXTON. SOONER OR LATER, I SEE EVERYONE.

SURE. AT THE END, ANYWAY.

THE END OF *WHAT?*

LIFE.

GIVE ME A BREAK. AND I SUPPOSE *YOU* KNOW WHAT HAPPENS WHEN YOU DIE.

OF COURSE I KNOW WHAT HAPPENS WHEN YOU DIE, SEXTON. I DO.

I'M DEATH.

YOU KNOW, I *THOUGHT* MAYBE YOU WERE KIND OF NICE AND KIND OF SMART. BUT I WAS *DEAD* WRONG. YOU'RE JUST AS CRAZY AS EVERYONE ELSE...

WELL, *I* THOUGHT YOU WERE SOMEONE *DUMB* ENOUGH TO GET STUCK UNDER A FRIDGE IN A GARBAGE DUMP. AND *I* WAS DEAD *RIGHT.*

SLAM

HULLO, ME BONNY BOY.

OH *JESUS,* ANOTHER CRAZY. OOOKAY... JUST PRETEND YOU DIDN'T SEE HER. YOU DON'T MAKE EYE CONTACT, IT'S OKAY...

LOOK UP. LOOK AWAY...

OW!

THERE WE GO ME BONNY BONNY BOY. AH YES, NEAT AS A NEW PIN. OH, MAD HETTIE'S LOST NONE OF HER TOUCH, HAS SHE? *OHHH* NO.

YOU WERE *WITH* HER, WEREN'T YOU? I CAN *SMELL* HER TOUCH ON YOU.

LADY, YOU CAN SMELL A *GARBAGE* DUMP ON ME MAYBE, BUT, UH--

YOU KNOW WHO I MEAN. DRESSES IN BLACK. LITTLE GYPSY DOOHICKE THING ROUND HER NECK. *YOU* KNOW.

DIDI?

WHATEVER.

UPSYDAISY DEARIO, IN MY EXPERIENCE, BROKEN BOTTLES IS SHARP AS BUGGERY, AND YOU'D *NOT* BE SO BONNY IF YOU GOT ONE IN THE FACE. *WOULD* YOU?

LADY--I *DON'T* KNOW WHAT YOUR PROBLEM IS, BU-BUT I'M NOT ANY *PART* OF THIS. IF YOU'VE GOT SOME *FIGHT* WITH DIDI, WELL...

BUTTON YOUR LIP AND SHUT YOUR FACE. UP THOSE STAIRS-- QUICK MARCH.

ONLY HERE A FEW HOURS, AND *ALREADY* SHE'S FOUND HERSELF A YOUNG MAN. FAST *MOVER*, ISN'T SHE?

YOU KNOW WHAT A MYOCLONIC *TWITCH* IS, BONNY BOY?

WELL, WHEN YOU'RE FALLING ASLEEP. AND YOUR MIND'S WANDERIN'. AND YOU'VE CROSSED OVER THE BOUNDARY OF SLEEPIN' AND WAKIN', AND YOU'RE BEGINNING TO ALMOST DREAM, AND IN THE DREAM YOU TAKE A STEP, OR MOVE AN ARM, AND IN REAL LIFE *IT* TWITCHES TOO. AND IT WAKES YOU BACK UP.

YOU EVER HAD *THAT?*

N-NO.

UH. Y-YEAH. YES. SURE.

THAT'S A MYOCLONIC TWITCH.

LADY, WHY ARE YOU *TELLING* ME THIS?

107

TWO REASONS, YOUNG FELLER-ME-LAD. ONE'S BECAUSE I WANT YOU TO KNOW THAT MAD HETTIE KNOWS A *LOT* OF THINGS. *SHE* WASN'T BORN YESTERDAY. *OH* NO.

SHE'S TWO HUNDRID AND FIFTY YEARS OLD, AND *SHE* KNOWS A THING OR TWO.

AND THE *OTHER* REASON? WELL, *THAT'S* TO DO WITH DYIN'.

BUT THAT'S NEITHER HERE NOR THERE, REELY. *IS* IT?

KNOCK ON THE DOOR.

AW, COME *ON*, LADY.

YOU KNOCK ON THAT DOOR OR THE SUN WILL BE SHINING ON PLACES INSIDE YOU THAT THE SUN DOESN'T USUALLY SHINE.

26

OH. IT'S *YOU* AGAIN.

AND IT'S *YOU*.

HMPH. WELL, WHAT *IS* IT, MAD HETTIE? WHAT DO *YOU* WANT?

THAT'S RIGHT. IT'S *ME*.

A HUNDRID YEARS AGO I MISSED YOU.

BUT I'VE HAD *PLENTY* OF TIME TO THINK SINCE THEN, AND I HAVEN'T MISSED YOU *THIS* TIME. OR MISSED THIS LITTLE LADDIE.

GET IN THERE, BONNY BOY.

I'M NOT LEAVING HIM OUT OF THIS. HE'S MY BARGAINING THING, *IN'T* HE?

LEAVE HIM OUT OF THIS, MAD HETTIE.

WHAT DO YOU *WANT* FROM ME?

27

A NIGHT TO REMEMBER

the high cost of living

MY NAME IS SEXTON FURNIVAL, AND I'VE HEARD ALL THE JOKES ABOUT IT YOU COULD EVER IMAGINE, AND FIVE HOURS AGO MY MOM THREW ME OUT OF THE APARTMENT.

IT'S THE MIDDLE OF JULY, AND SHE'S SPRING-CLEANING, BUT THAT'S SYLVIA FOR YOU.

SHE DIDN'T THROW ME OUT FOR GOOD; I CAN GO BACK WHEN SHE FINISHES CLEANING. IT'S JUST WHEN SYLVIA GOES MANIC IT'S A GOOD IDEA TO KEEP OUT OF HER WAY. 4:00 AM SHE COULD BE UP REPAINTING THE DOORFRAMES OR SOMETHING.

RIGHT NOW, I'M WALKING DOWN A SIDEWALK NEXT TO A GIRL I MET ON A GARBAGE DUMP WHO MAKES MY MOTHER LOOK LIKE THE UTTER PROTOTYPE OF SANE NORMALITY.

HER NAME'S DIDI. SHE SAYS SHE'S THE HUMAN INCARNATION OF THE SPIRIT OF DEATH, OR WORDS TO THAT EFFECT. SHE'S ABOUT MY AGE. HER FAMILY WAS KILLED RECENTLY IN A CAR CRASH.

SHE'S WEARING A DUMB HAT AND A TERMINALLY PERKY SMILE AND SHE SAYS WE'RE GOING OFF TO FIND A REALLY GOOD PARTY.

WHICH IS KIND OF A RELIEF, BECAUSE FIVE MINUTES AGO I WAS STANDING IN HER APARTMENT WITH A REALLY PRETTY SHARP BROKEN GLASS BOTTLE PRESSED INTO THE SIDE OF MY FACE.

THE BOTTLE WAS BEING HELD BY YE ANOTHER CRAZY PERSON, ONLY THIS ONE SMELLED LIKE A STORM-DRAIN, AND SHE SAID SHE WAS HUNDREDS OF YEARS OLD, AND SHE WAS GOING TO CUT OFF MY NOSE IF DIDI DIDN'T HELP HER FIND HER HEART.

I HATE IT WHEN THINGS BECOME SURR

DIDI SAID, "YOU REALLY WANT ME TO FIND YOUR HEART?"

COURSE I DO. YOU FINK I COME UP HERE FOR ME *HEALTH* OR SOMEFING?

I PUT THE LITTEL BUGGER SOMEWHERE SAFE AS HOUSES, I DID. SOMEWHERE NO ONE WOULD FIND IT, 'SPECIALLY NOT *YOU.*

YOU DON'T REACH A RIPE OLD AGE WITHOUT KNOWING A TRICK OR TWO. ANYWAY, IT'S *TRADITIONAL,* HIDIN' YER HEART.

LET ME GET THIS STRAIGHT. YOU'VE HIDDEN IT FROM *ME.* AND YOU WANT *ME* TO FIND IT FOR *YOU?*

OKAY. I'LL LOOK FOR IT. BUT THERE'S STUFF OF MY OWN I WANT TO DO AS WELL, TONIGHT.

ANY IDEA WHERE YOU *LEFT* IT?

MAYHAP I PLACED IT IN A DUCK EGG, INSIDE A DUCK, INSIDE A WELL, IN A CASTLE, ON AN ISLAND, SURROUNDED BY A LAKE OF FIRE, GUARDED BY A HUNDRED DRAGONS EACH LARGER AND MORE FEROCIOUS THAN THE LAST...

AND MAYBE YOU *DIDN'T?*

WELL, IT'S BEEN A LONG TIME, LOVEY. ME MIND GOES WANDERIN'.

MAD HETTIE?

YES, DEARIO?

THERE'S COKE IN THE FRIDGE, COFFEE IN THE PERCOLATOR, AND YOU CAN HELP YOURSELF TO FOOD.

...SO WHAT HAPPENED *THEN*?

MY BROTHER, HE WRITE ME LETTER, HE SAY, IS *WONDERFUL* COUNTRY, BETTER YOU COME OUT HERE PRETTY GODDAMN QUICK.

SO I *COME* OUT HERE, AND I SAY TO MY BROTHER, HEY, WHAT *NOW*, AND HE SAYS, YOU *DRIVE* PRETTY GODDAMN GOOD, MAYBE YOU SHOULD DRIVE A *TAXI*.

WELL, *I* THINK YOU'RE A VERY GOOD DRIVER, TOO.

OVER THERE--WHAT ARE ALL THOSE PEOPLE GOING IN THERE FOR?

I'VE BEEN THERE. IT'S CALLED *THE UNDERCUT*. IT'S TOO HOT AND YOU CAN'T BREATHE. THEY HAVE SOME GOOD BANDS PLAYING FROM TIME TO TIME, THOUGH.

STOP! STOP! THIS'S WHERE WE'RE GOING, MISTER TAXI DRIVER.

OKAY. I'M GLAD WE *FIND* IT SO EASY.

15.00

THANKS. WHAT DO I OWE YOU?

IS A PRESENT. IS FOR NOTHING.

THANK YOU.

SEXTON, SAY *THANK YOU* TO THE NICE MAN.

YOU PEOPLE JUST DON'T *DO* THAT. I MEAN, NEW YORK CAB DRIVERS JUST DON'T *GIVE* FREE RIDES. I DON'T *GET* IT.

HER, I LIKE.

YOU, I *DON'T* LIKE. SO YOU CAN GIVE ME THE TIP. TWO BUCKS.

UM. *WHY* DO YOU HAVE A BULB OF GARLIC HANGING FROM YOUR MIRROR?

IT KEEP *BAD* THINGS AWAY.

WHEN PEOPLE DO NICE THINGS, SEXTON, YOU SHOULD *ALWAYS* SAY THANKYOU, IT MAKES LIFE AN AWFUL LOT EASIER.

DO YOU *KNOW* ANY OF THESE PEOPLE?

YOU *KIDDING?* I DON'T KNOW ANY FASHION VICTIMS.

HI, SEXTON!

JESUS. HI, HAZEL. WHAT ARE *YOU* DOING HERE?

FOX IS PLAYING TONIGHT.

PLAYING *WHAT?* I THOUGHT FOXGLOVE WROTE LIKE, SHORT STORIES OR SOMETHING.

I THINK SHE GOT TIRED OF NOT *SELLING* ANY. THIS IS HER FIRST REAL GIG THAT ANYONE'S GIVING HER ANY MONEY FOR. I WOULDN'T HAVE COME DOWN OTHERWISE. WHAT WITH THE *BUMP* AND EVERYTHING.

SO WHO'S YOUR *FRIEND?*

THIS IS DIDI. NOBODY MAKES HER PAY FOR ANYTHING.

WHEN'S IT DUE?

ANY DAY NOW.

NEAT. THIS YOUR FIRST?

AND LAST, PROBABLY. I'M HAZEL. I USED TO COOK IN SYLVIA'S RESTAURANT.

SYLVIA'S MY MOTHER. SHE SAYS HAZEL WAS THE BEST CHEF THEY EVER *HAD.*

I WAS OKAY. LOOK, DO YOU GUYS WANT TO COME AND SEE FOXGLOVE? I MEAN, SHE'LL APPRECIATE ALL THE SUPPORT SHE GETS.

I'M ON THE DOOR, PLUS TWO. SO I CAN GET YOU IN FREE. IF YOU WANT TO COME...?

YOU DARLING, WE'D LOVE THAT.

8

I LIKE YOUR *HAT.* BUT FOX IS THE ONE IN THE FAMILY WITH FASHION SENSE. I WOULDN'T *DARE.*

HAVE YOU KNOWN SEXTON LONG?

I FOUND HIM ON A GARBAGE DUMP THIS AFTERNOON.

THAT'S REALLY FUNNY.

I'M HAZEL McNAMARA. I'M WITH FOXGLOVE, THESE TWO ARE WITH ME,

YEAH. YOU'RE DOWN ON THE LIST. GO ON IN.

I DON'T *GET* IT: SINCE I'VE BEEN WITH YOU, YOU HAVEN'T PAID FOR *ANYTHING.* I WISH *I* COULD LIVE FOR FREE.

NOBODY LIVES FOR FREE, SEXTON. ESPECIALLY NOT ME.

I'VE GOT TEN DOLLARS AND TWO CENTS ON ME.

GREAT. *THAT'LL* BUY US PLENTY OF DRINKS.

HERE, SEXTON, I'LL PAY. GET ME AN ORANGE JUICE, AND YOU, DIDI?

I'LL HAVE A COKE.

GET YOURSELF WHATEVER YOU WANT, SEXTON. AS LONG AS IT DOESN'T GET YOU CARDED.

I'M GLAD SEXTON'S GOT A *FRIEND*. I MEAN, I'VE KNOWN HIM SINCE HE WAS TWELVE.

HE WAS A NICE KID.

SO DO YOU STILL COOK?

NOT PROFESSIONALLY. A LOT OF STUFF WENT DOWN LAST YEAR. WHEN I GOT PREGNANT, WE *LOST* THE PLACE WE WERE STAYING, AND WE WOUND UP MOVING IN WITH MY MOTHER, AND FOX GOT REALLY SERIOUS ABOUT WRITING. AND *THEN* SHE WANTED TO START PERFORMING TOO.

OOH! HE KICKED! YOU WANT TO FEEL HIM *KICKING*?

SURE.

WON'T TAKE YOU BACKSTAGE OR ANYTHING. FOX 'LL BE THROWING UP. SHE DOESN'T LIKE PEOPLE 'ROUND WHILE SHE HYPERVENTILATES AND PUKES. BUT AFTER THE SHOW, IF YOU WANT...

I CHOSE TO HAVE A BABY BUT I'M GLAD I HAD A CHOICE.

OOH! HE DID IT AGAIN.

I GOT THE ULTRASOUND THINGIE. THAT'S HOW WE KNOW IT'S A BOY.

MY MOM LOANED US THE MONEY FOR ALL THIS BABY STUFF. IT'S SIX *THOUSAND* DOLLARS. YOU *KNOW* THAT? SIX THOUSAND.

'RANGE JUICE. 'OKE. YOUR 'CHANGE.

THANKS, SEXTON. WHAT ARE YOU DRINKING?

GINGER ALE.

GOOD. HEY, YOU KNOW THE *WORST* THING ABOUT BEING PREGNANT?

OH GOD. THIS ISN'T ONE OF THOSE *GROSS* THINGS, IS IT?

LIKE HAVING TO EAT THE AFTERBIRTH OR SOMETHING?

SHUT UP, BRAT. NO, IT'S NOT SMOKING. I HAVEN'T HAD A CIGARETTE FOR SEVEN *MONTHS*.

I TELL YOU, AS SOON AS BABY MCNAMARA BREATHES HIS FIRST BREATH, I'M GOING TO START INHALING SMOKE AGAIN.

LISTEN, I'M GOING BACKSTAGE TO SAY HI TO FOX. I'LL CATCH YOU TWO LATER.

10

SHE'S OKAY. SYLVIA GOT PRETTY MAD AT HER WHEN SHE QUIT.

SHE'S REALLY NICE.

LISTEN-- THAT OLD CRAZY LADY...

MAD HETTIE?

YEAH. ARE YOU GOING TO CALL THE POLICE, OR ANYTHING?

OF COURSE NOT. I PROMISED HER WE'D GO AND FIND HER HEART.

I FIGURED YOU WERE I DON'T KNOW. HUMORING HER. I MEAN, EVEN YOU SAID SHE'S MAD.

SURE, COMPLETELY LOOPY. BUT SHE'S STILL TWO HUNDRED AND FIFTY YEARS OLD. AND SHE NEEDS HER HEART BACK.

I WONDER HOW SHE GOT TO NEW YORK. PROBABLY STOWED AWAY ON A SHIP, OR SOMETHING, AND SHE GETS REALLY SEASICK. POOR LOVE.

I'M MEANT TO FEEL SORRY FOR A CRAZY OLD LADY WHO NEARLY CUT MY NOSE OFF?

IF YOU KNOW SOMEONE REALLY WELL IT'S HARD TO BE MAD AT THEM FOR VERY LONG.

AND YOU KNOW HER REALLY WELL.

I KNOW EVERYBODY REALLY WELL.

I...YOU REALLY PISS ME OFF. YOU KNOW THAT?

I DON'T KNOW WHY I'M HANGING OUT WITH YOU.

BECAUSE I WANT YOU TO. SHUSH. SHE'S STARTING.

HI, EVERYONE. WELCOME TO THE UNDERCUT. HER NAME'S FOXGLOVE. THIS IS HER FIRST GIG. TREAT HER KIND.

UH...GOOD EVENING. THIS SONG IS CALLED DONNA'S DREAM. IT'S ABOUT SOME PEOPLE I KNEW. AT LEAST ONE OF THEM IS DEAD.

THANKS. THIS NEXT SONG WAS INSPIRED BY SOMETHING MY FRIEND *WANDA* ONCE SAID TO ME. *SHE'S DEAD TOO.*

MAYBE IT'S *CONTAGIOUS.*

IT'S CALLED *TRACKS.*

IF SOMEWHERE IN THE DARK I AM ALONE WILL YOU COME TO ME, BRINGING ME YOUR LIGHT...

WOW. SHE'S PRETTY *GOOD*, ISN'T SHE?

I DUNNO. I MEAN MICHELE SHOCKED DID THE NAIF GAL WITH AN ACOUSTIC GUITAR SHTICK ALREADY, AND DID IT BETTER. AND SUZANNE VEGA DID THE WISTFUL INTELLECTUAL WITH A DREAM DIARY BIT. SHE DOESN'T SAY ANYTHING *NEW.*

WHAT *ARE* YOU? A *CRITIC* OR SOMETHING?

NO. I'M WITH A RECORD COMPANY. I'M ONLY OUT HERE FOR A WEEK. I'M FROM *L.A.*

YEAH, I BEEN THERE. WHAT LABEL?

XERXES. WE'RE PART OF--

YEAH, I KNOW. YOU KNOW MY DAD? STEVE FURNIVAL?

THE *LAWYER?* HE'S YOUR *FATHER?* HEY, THAT'S *GREAT.*

MM.

SO, UH... YOU *LIKE* HER, HUH? YOU DON'T THINK SHE'D BE TOO, LIKE, *MORBID* FOR THE KIDS?

I'M A KID. SHE'S MORBID ENOUGH FOR *ME.*

YEAH? STEVE FURNIVAL'S SON, HUH?

AND YOU THINK SHE'S *GOT* SOMETHING?

HEY! KID!

HERE'S MY CARD. LOOK ME UP WHEN YOU'RE IN L.A. OKAY?

MAYBE.

13

YOU LOOKING FOR SOMEONE?

YEAH. THE GIRL I CAME HERE WITH.

OH. WHAT'S YOUR NAME?

SEXTON.

NEAT NAME.

NOT REALLY.

UH. IS YOUR HAIR *REALLY* THAT COLOR?

SWEET CHILD. *NOBODY'S* HAIR IS REALLY THIS COLOR.

DON'T CALL ME THAT.

WELL, HOW OLD ARE YOU?

SIXTEEN. *YOU?*

A WOMAN'S AGE IS HER OWN AFFAIR. AND WHAT ARE *YOU* GOING TO BE WHEN YOU GROW UP, SWEET CHILD?

DEAD.

AH, LIVE FAST, LOVE HARD, LEAVE A BEAUTIFUL CORPSE.

NOT REALLY. MORE LIVE DULL, AND THINK, *WHY BOTHER,* AND LEAVE A NOTE SAYING GOODBYE.

HM. DO YOU *MEAN* THAT?

SURE.

YOU REALLY *ARE* A CHILD. YOU KNOW, *ENNUI* IS INSUFFICIENT REASON TO COMMIT SUICIDE.

14

I...HAD A FRIEND WHO WAS BADLY ABUSED, SEXUALLY, BETWEEN THE AGES OF 12 AND 15, BY HER FATHER, AND BY FIVE OF HER FATHER'S FRIENDS.

THE FAMILY *FICTION* WAS THAT SHE--MY *FRIEND*-- LIKED HUNTING, WHICH WAS WHY HER FATHER WOULD TAKE HER OFF WITH HIM AND HIS BUDDIES ON THEIR CAMPING TRIPS.

THEY,...

THEY MADE HER DO A *LOT* OF THINGS SHE DIDN'T LIKE.

HER FATHER WAS THE MAYOR OF THE TOWN IN QUESTION, AND ONE OF THE FIVE FRIENDS WAS POLICE CHIEF. THERE WAS NO ONE SHE COULD GO TO.

AND ONE DAY IT ALL GOT TOO *MUCH*. AND SHE GOT HER DADDY'S BIG OLD HUNTING KNIFE, AND SHE LOCKED HERSELF IN THE BATHROOM, AND SHE STARTED TO SLICE.

AND WHEN SHE WOKE UP IN THE HOSPITAL, WITH BANDAGES ALL DOWN HER ARMS, SHE WAS... *SOME*HOW... *STILL* GLAD TO BE ALIVE.

IS THAT IT?

YES.

SO WHAT HAPPENED TO HER, THEN?

I EXPECT SHE CAME OUT TO THE BIG CITY. DOESN'T EVERYONE?

YEAH. WELL, THANKS FOR THE STORY. I'M GOING TO SEE HOW MY *FRIEND* IS DOING.

HI, SEXTON.

HMP. CAN I TALK TO YOU A SECOND, DIDI?

SURE. BE RIGHT BACK, THEO.

DO YOU KNOW WHO THAT GUY IS? THE GUY YOU'RE TALKING TO?

SURE. HIS NAME'S THEO.

I KNOW HIS NAME'S THEO. HE'S AT MY SCHOOL. HE'S CRAZY. I MEAN, YOU MUSTN'T TALK TO HIM.

ARE YOU TRYING TO TELL ME WHO I CAN AND CAN'T TALK TO, NOW?

WELL. YES.

SO IT'S OKAY FOR YOU TO TALK TO THAT HENNA WORSHIPPER WITH THE LONG GLOVES, BUT IT'S NOT OKAY FOR ME TO CHAT WITH SOMEONE?

YES. NO. LOOK, HE'S REALLY, WELL, I MEAN, I DON'T KNOW. I MEAN. YOU HEAR STUFF. YOU KNOW?

HEY, BABY. YOU GONNA BE LONG?

NO. JUST A SECOND.

DID YOU HEAR THAT? HE CALLED YOU BABY. LOOK. HE'S A CREEP, OKAY?

16

THERE'S NO DOOR HANDLE.

FORGET THAT AND COME OVER HERE. I THINK THEO'S BADLY HURT.

THAT'S A PROBLEM? I THINK ANYBODY WHO SAYS "NOT" AT THE END OF A SENTENCE DESERVES TO BE BADLY HURT.

I DON'T WANT TO HEAR THAT STUFF, SEXTON. THIS IS A REAL PERSON YOU'RE TALKING ABOUT, AND HE'S NOT BREATHING PROPERLY, AND I'M SURE HE'S DONE A LOT WORSE THAN SAYING NOT, BUT I'M TELLING YOU, SOMETIMES YOU REALLY PISS ME OFF, AND RIGHT NOW THAT SMART-ALECK SHIT IS THE LAST THING I NEED TO HEAR, OKAY?

UH...

UH, WHAT'S WRONG WITH HIM?

DO I LOOK LIKE A DOCTOR? HIS HEAD'S BLEEDING. MAYBE HE'S CONCUSSED. AND I THINK HIS NOSE IS BROKEN.

NOW, GET OVER HERE AND GIVE ME A HAND, AND SHUT UP.

I THINK YOU BETTER HOLD HIS HEAD UP. THERE'S BLOOD COMING FROM HIS NOSE, AND HE COULD CHOKE...

OKAY.

I'M SORRY I SNAPPED AT YOU, SEXTON. I... I SHOULDN'T HAVE COME DOWN HERE. OR BROUGHT YOU WITH.

SOMETIMES I GET A BIT COCKY, YOU KNOW? AND.. WELL, I MADE MISTAKE.

UM. THAT'S OKAY.

YEAH. WELL.

KRRRRRRRCHHHHHH

WHAT WAS THAT?

THAT WAS. WELL, YOU CAN LET GO OF HIS HEAD, SEXTON. THAT WAS A DEATH RATTLE.

UH, REALLY? I THOUGHT THAT WAS JUST A, THING. SOMETHING PEOPLE SAY.

HEY, IF YOU WERE LIKE, *REALLY* THE SPIRIT OF DEATH, SHOULDN'T YOU HAVE BEEN HERE FOR HIM WHEN HE DIED?

WELL, IT IS. IT'S SOMETHING THEY SAY AT THE END.

I WAS HERE, SEXTON.

OH YEAH.

I'VE...NEVER SEEN A DEAD BODY BEFORE.

I HAVE.

THAT MAN. HE'S GOING TO KILL US TOO, ISN'T HE?

SORT OF.

WHAT DOES THAT MEAN?

WELL, HE PROBABLY PLANS TO KILL *YOU*. NOTHING PERSONAL, BUT YOU'VE SEEN TOO MUCH.

DEAD MEN TELL NO TALES, HUH?

EVERYBODY TELLS TALES, SEXTON. IT'S JUST THE DEAD TALK MORE QUIETLY THAN OTHER PEOPLE.

BUT HE WON'T KILL *YOU*?

2

PROBABLY NOT IMMEDIATELY. I'M TOO VALUABLE.

I'M *HUNGRY.*

POOR MAD HETTIE.

POOR MAD HETTIE? WHAT'S *THAT* SUPPOSED TO MEAN?

WELL, SHE TRUSTED US TO GET HER HEART BACK. AND I THINK WE MESSED UP.

YOU'RE CRAZY, YOU KNOW THAT?

JUST BECAUSE OTHER PEOPLE ARE CRAZY TOO, DOESN'T MEAN YOU'RE NOT CRAZY.

HEY. I PROMISED YOU A NIGHT TO REMEMBER, DIDN'T I?

YOU SHOULD TAKE YOUR *MIND* OFF IT. THERE'S MORE OLD MAGAZINES HERE THAN IN A DENTIST'S WAITING ROOM. WHY DON'T YOU *READ* SOMETHING?

HUH?

OR PLAY WITH SOME OF THE *TOYS.* THEY AREN'T *ALL* BROKEN. SEE THIS CLOWN?

IF YOU KNOCK HIM *DOWN,* HE JUST *BOUNCES* RIGHT UP AGAIN.

LIKE *US.* WE'LL GET OUT OF THIS MESS. IT'LL BE FINE.

YOU'LL SEE.

WATCH *THIS!*

26

l i v i n

t h e   h i g h   c o s t   o f

the high cost of

WHIST, WHIST. AH, BUT THIS IS THE LIFE, *MAD HETTIE* ME PET, AND *WHO'S* A CLEVER OLD BIDDIE? INDEED, 'TIS YERSELF AND *NO* MISTAKE.

NOW ALL WE NEEDS IS A CUPPA AND LIFE'S A MERRIE FING INDEED. ANY MINUTE NOW THEY'LL BE RETURNIN' WIV OUR HEART, ME DEARIO.

AND THEN I'LL DANCE. *OH* HOW I'LL DANCE.

OH BUT WHEN AND I WAS A TIPPY TINY GIRL *SINGIN' RATS AN' MICE AND DAISIES-OH WITH EYES OF BLUE AND PRETTY YELLOW CURLS SINGIN' NEWTS AN' TOADS AN' SNAKES AN' SQUIRRELS AN' BATS AN' HERRINGS AND DAISIES-OH...*

TCH. WHERE'S THE TEA, *EH?* WHERE'S THE TEAPOTS? WHERE'S THE KETTLE?

FLOATIN' IN BOSTON HARBOR, NO DOUBT, WIV ALL THEM YOUNG GENTLEMEN DRESSED AS SAVAGES. *I* REMEMBERS.

HO YUSS, HWELCOME TO HAMERICA, MED 'ETTIE. 'EV SOME CAWFFEE.

TCH.

YOU KNOW, WHEN I *SAW* THIS IN THE WAREHOUSE, I JUST HAD TO BUY ONE FOR MYSELF. ASK YOURSELF-- WHERE ELSE ARE YOU GOING TO FIND ZIRCONS AT A PRICE LIKE THIS?

THAT'S $19.95 FOR THE BRACELET, THE EARRINGS *AND* THE KEY-CHAIN. LET'S TAKE A CALL.

HELLO, CALLER, WHO'S ON THE LINE?

THIS IS BERNICE IN FLORIDA. I WAS GOING TO BED, BUT THEN I SAW THE LOVELY JEWELRY.

AND ARE YOU A REGULAR HOME SHOPPING VIEWER, BERNICE?

UH-HUH.

AND HOW MANY OF THESE BEAUTIFUL BRACELET SETS ARE YOU BUYING?

TWO. ONE FOR ME, AND ONE FOR MY MOTHER-IN-LAW.

KNOCK KNOCK

YOU KNOW THESE ARE *REAL* ZIRCONS, BERNICE?

YOU GOT ANY *TEA?* PROPER TEA, NONE OF THIS HERBAL MUCK?

WHAT ARE YOU? *CRAZY* OR SOMETHING?

MAD AS A PORRIDGE-KNIFE. YOU CAN CALL ME *HETTIE,* LOVEY. GOT ANY *TEA?*

2

BONNIE BOY? WAS IT *YOU* PUT THESE AGGIES ALL OVER THE FLOOR?

AGGIES?

THESE FINGS.

UM, YES.

WELL, *THAT* WAS A BLOODY *STUPID* THING TO DO. YOU COULD OF *KILLED* SOMEONE!

MAD HETTIE? WHAT ARE *YOU* DOING HERE?

SHE READ IT IN THE TEA LEAVES.

HUH?

SHE CAME UP TO MY PLACE TO GET SOME TEA. I HAD SOME ENGLISH BREAKFAST TEA. MY SON LARRY SENT IT LAST CHRISTMAS, IN A HAMPER. CHRISTMAS PUDDING AND EVERYTHING.

7

I MADE IT MESELF. YOU *CAN'T* TRUST AMERICANS TO MAKE A PROPER CUP LIKE *I* LIKE IT, *NO* OFFENSE, LOVE.

AND THEN SHE SAID THAT DIDI WAS BEING HELD PRISONER SOMEWHERE DOWN-TOWN.

YOU READ THAT WE WERE *HERE* ... IN *TEA LEAVES?*

MORE OR LESS. WE BIN LOOKIN' FOR YOU SINCE JUST GONE MIDNIGHT.

THERE'S A LOT OF PLACES ROUND HERE YOU *COULD* OF BIN. THAT'S THE *TROUBLE* WITH TEA LEAVES. THEY'RE GOOD FOR THE *GENERAL* BUT BUGGER ALL USE FOR THE *SPECIFICS.*

LIVER AND ENTRAILS, NOW, *THAT'S* BEST FOR SPECIFICS.

DIDI GIRL. THAT *BOY* DOWN THERE. IS HE *DEAD?*

YES, MRS. ROBBINS.

WHAT'S HE DOING *DEAD?*

THE MAN WHO LOCKED US UP HERE. HE KILLED HIM.

HIS NAME'S THEO. WAS THEO. IT WAS HIS FAULT. *HE* GOT US TO COME HERE.

YOU GOING TO CALL THE POLICE?

I SUPPOSE WE *HAVE* TO.

YOU OUT OF YOUR *MIND?* AT SIX IN THE MORNING? WITH A DEAD BODY ON THE FLOOR?

BUT THERE WAS THIS CRAZY BLIND MAN. HE TOOK DIDI'S ANKH. HE WAS GOING TO KILL ME. KILL *BOTH* OF US.

8

WHAT TIME IS IT?

BREAKFAST TIME ON A REALLY MOST EXCELLENT SUMMER'S DAY. YOU KNOW WHAT *WE* NEED?

I HAVE NO IDEA WHAT *YOU* THINK *I* NEED. *YOU* NEED SUBTITLES. OR SOME KIND OF INSTRUCTION MANUAL.

WE NEED BREAKFAST. IN HERE.

A BAGEL, PLEASE. WITH LOX AND CREAM CHEESE. AND A GLASS OF ORANGE JUICE.

SCRAMBLED EGGS AND HASH BROWNS, PLEASE.

YOU WANT THE BEST LOX, OR THE CHEAP STUFF? *ME?* I WOULDN'T BE CAUGHT *DEAD* EATING THE CHEAP STUFF. BUT NU, IT'S *YOUR* BREAKFAST, *I'M* GOING TO TELL *YOU* WHAT TO EAT?

I'LL HAVE BEST, PLEASE.

I *LOVE* FOOD. FOOD IS *SO* GREAT. I MEAN, IT'S *SO* MUCH MORE FUN THAN PHOTOSYNTHE-SIS...

...OR HAVING A POWER PACK IN YOUR BACK, OR BATHING IN LIQUID CRYSTALS, OR ANY OF THOSE THINGS.

LIKE YOU'D *KNOW?*

OH, I'VE BEEN DOING THIS ONE-DAY-A-CENTURY BIT FOR *QUITE* A LONG TIME NOW...

HOW WERE YOU FREED?

10

WE WALKED OUT.

BUT YOU WERE *POWERLESS.* I HAVE YOUR ANKH. I *HAVE* IT.

CAN I HAVE IT *BACK?*

OH NO. *I* HAVE YOUR *SIGIL* OF POWER. I HAVE YOUR ANKH. WITH IT I WILL UNLOCK *ALL* SECRETS OF LIFE AND DEATH.

YOU DON'T HAVE *ME.*

YOU WILL NOT ESCAPE ME.

OH, I'M SURE WE'LL MEET AGAIN. *EVENTUALLY.*

HEY! YOU! MISTER SO-WELL-DRESSED YOU'RE MAKING ME FEEL EMBARRASSED!

SO WHAT ARE *YOU* DOING IN HERE? LOOKING FOR A *HANDOUT?*

I AM THE EREMITE. MINE IS THE GLORY. MINE IS RIGHTEOUSNESS.

KIDS, I'M SORRY ABOUT THIS. *LOOK*, FELLA. I DON'T KNOW WHAT YOUR PROBLEM IS, BUT MAYBE YOU WANT TO HAVE IT OUTSIDE, HUH? IF IT WAS *ME*, I'D SAY *STAY, ENJOY,* MAYBE WE COULD HAVE A *PARTY,* BUT IT'S NOT JUST ME, IT'S THE CUSTOMERS.

BUT SHE IS *DEATH!* HER *TOUCH* IS DEATH. HER *FLESH* IS *CORRUPTION* AND HER *EYES* BREED *MAGGOTS.*

YEAH, YEAH. C'MON. OUTSIDE.

BUT SHE WILL *NOT* TRIUMPH! I HAVE HER *SIGIL!* I SHALL *CONQUER* DEATH AND BEND HER TO MY *BIDDING!*

UH-HUH. SURE YOU WILL. *SUUUURE* YOU HAVE. SURE YOU DO...NOW. *OUT.*

HEY, KIDS, I'M *SORRY* ABOUT THAT. MOSTLY WE DON'T GET THAT SORT IN HERE. HE'S A PRETTY *SCARY* ONE, HUH?

IT'S OKAY. THANK YOU F MAKING HI GO OUTSID

HE BEEN BOTHERING YOU FOR LONG?

HOURS.

HM.

C'MON THROUGH HERE. YOU CAN GO OUT THROUGH THE BACK.

WHAT ABOUT BREAKFAST? WE HAVEN'T PAID YOU.

HEY, IT WAS ON THE HOUSE. GOD FORBID YOU SHOULD TELL PEOPLE I DIDN'T TAKE CARE OF YOU. I'M JUST SORRY ABOUT THE MESHUGGENER.

THANK YOU.

FREE BREAKFAST. UH-HUH. YOU REALLY NEVER PAY FOR ANYTHING.

I TOLD YOU. I PAY. EVERYBODY PAYS.

HE THINKS THAT THING OF YOURS HAS POWER.

HE'S RIGHT, OF COURSE. IT'S A SYMBOL OF LIFE; AND SYMBOLS HAVE POWER.

MAYBE NOT THE WAY HE THINKS, THOUGH.

ARE YOU GOING TO TRY TO GET IT BACK FROM HIM?

GET IT BACK? WHY?

WELL. HE SEEMED TO THINK IT WAS IMPORTANT. YOU BOTH DID.

IT'S THE MOST IMPORTANT THING IN THE WHOLE UNIVERSE.

12

JUST *GIVE* IT TO HER. GET IT OVER WITH. YOU'RE GOING TO *ANYWAY*, AND THE SUSPENSE IS GOING TO KILL ME.

YOU CRAZY OR SOMETHIN'?

HOW MUCH IS THIS ONE?

TO YOU?

OF COURSE TO ME.

TEN BUCKS EVEN.

IT'S NOT REAL *SILVER*, IS IT?

FOR TEN BUCKS YOU'RE LUCKY IT'S REAL *METAL*.

IT'S A NICE ONE, THANKS.

SO THAT CLEANS YOU OUT, HUH?

MM. I GOT A COUPLE OF CENTS LEFT.

13

SEXTON? ISN'T YOUR MOTHER GOING TO BE WORRIED ABOUT YOU BY NOW?

SYLVIA? SHE WOULDN'T NOTICE IF I WENT TO THE MOON.

SHE PROBABLY WOULD. MOTHERS *NOTICE* THAT KIND OF THING.

IF YOU'RE *REALLY* DEATH... WHAT HAPPENS WHEN PEOPLE DIE? I MEAN, DO YOU BELIEVE IN HEAVEN AND HELL AND THAT STUFF? OR REINCARNATION? OR NIRVANA? OR DO WE JUST BLINK OUT LIKE LIGHT BULBS?

IF I *WAS* REALLY DEATH, DO YOU THINK I'D TELL *YOU*?

I DON'T KNOW *WHAT* YOU'RE GOING TO DO ANY MORE. IF A HUNDRED PENGUINS CAME DOWN BROADWAY AND DID A LITTLE DANCE WITH YOU I DON'T THINK I'D EVEN *BLINK*.

SEXTON? YOU KNOW, *UNDERNEATH*, YOU'RE PRETTY OKAY.

YEAH? WELL, UNDERNEATH, YOU'RE...

YES?

HAVE YOU EVER NOTICED HOW MUCH *BETTER* EVERYTHING SEEMS AFTER A GOOD BREAKFAST?

URE.

I'M GOING UP TO CENTRAL PARK. YOU WANT TO GO HOME NOW?

IT'S NOT THAT I EN*JOY* HANGING AROUND WITH YOU OR ANYTHING. BUT IF I WENT HOME. WELL, HOW WOULD I KNOW HOW ALL THIS IS GOING TO *END*?

ANYWAY, HOW ARE YOU GOING TO CONVINCE MAD HETTIE YOU'VE FOUND HER HEART?

OH, SHE'LL KNOW.

14

MY FATHER USED TO TAKE ME TO CENTRAL PARK. THAT WAS BEFORE SYLVIA AND STEVE DIVORCED.

IT'S FUNNY. I MEAN, I WAS ONLY ABOUT SIX OR SEVEN WHEN THEY SEPARATED. *MOST* OF WHAT I REMEMBER WAS JUST SITTING IN MY BEDROOM IN THE DARK, *TRYING* TO *STOP* THEM FROM SPLITTING UP.

TRYING? HOW?

JUST TRYING TO DO... *MAGIC*, I SUPPOSE. I'D SIT AND PRAY, AND CONCENTRATE, AND JUST TRY TO *STOP* THEM. I WAS TRYING TO MAKE THEM *LOVE* EACH OTHER AGAIN.

I MEAN, THEY DIDN'T EVEN *SPEAK* TO EACH OTHER. ONLY SOMETIMES STEVE WOULDN'T COME *HOME* AT NIGHT, AND SOMETIMES SYLVIA WOULD JUST SIT AROUND AND CRY, AND THEY DIDN'T *LOVE* EACH OTHER AND THERE WASN'T ANYTHING I COULD *DO* ABOUT IT.

AND ONE DAY STEVE WALKED OUT OF THE HOUSE AND HE DIDN'T COME BACK. *THAT* WAS WHEN I KNEW THERE *WASN'T* ANY MAGIC.

AND I WENT INTO MY ROOM AND LAY ON THE BED AND WISHED I WAS *DEAD*. AND THAT DIDN'T HAPPEN EITHER.

WOW-- SEXTON? DID YOU SEE THAT *RAT*?

THEY'RE ALL *OVER* THIS PLACE. LIKE SQUIRRELS. I SAW A THING ON TV ABOUT IT.

MY *SISTER* HAS RATS. SHE LOVES THEM DEEPLY. LIKE ME AND SLIM AND WANDSWORTH.

HM?

THE *GOLDFISH*.

SEXTON?

YEAH?

I HAD A GOOD TIME TODAY.

YOU *LIKE* BEING LOCKED UP IN WARE-HOUSES AND BEING THREATENED BY LOONIES, AND...

NO. I *DIDN'T* LIKE THAT, BUT....IT'S PART OF THE WHOLE THING. AND THERE *IS* A WHOLE THING OUT THERE. AND IT'S ALL PART OF LIVING.

THE *GOOD* BITS AND THE *BAD* BITS AND THE *DULL* BITS AND THE *PAINFUL* BITS--

OKAY. I GET THE POINT. THE WHOLE THING, RIGHT. VERY PROFOUND.

I LIKE THIS PLACE. IT'S A ITTLE BIT OF PEACE AND QUIET. AND I LIKE *HER.*

I LIKE YOU TOO.

IT'S REALLY NICE, ISN'T IT?

HERE.

WHAT'S *THIS* FOR?

IT'S WHAT I'VE GOT LEFT. IT'S FOR *YOU.*

THANKS. I'LL USE IT AS A DEPOSIT FOR MY FIRST CAR.

OH, AND THIS IS FOR MAD HETTIE.

WHY CAN'T YOU GIVE IT TO HER *YOURSELF?*

SEXTON?

I HAD A LOVELY DAY. THANKS.

DID I?

SHE ESCAPED ME, THEN.

IF YOU HURT HER, I'LL KILL YOU.

HA HA HA HA HA HA HA HA

I CAN NO LONGER HURT HER, BOY, IF EVER I COULD. NO MAN CAN.

GIVE ME THE PENNIES.

SHE NEEDS A DOCTOR.

CALL EVERY DOCTOR IN CHRISTENDOM, BOY, AND HE'LL DO NOTHING FOR HER. GIVE ME THE PENNIES.

THESE?

THERE, BOY. THAT'S THE COST OF A LIFE.

I CAN WAIT. SHE CANNOT ESCAPE ME FOREVER, BOY.

ONE DAY I TOO SHALL DIE.

ONE DAY...

18

OH, IT WAS *WONDERFUL*. IT WAS FILLED WITH *PEOPLE*. I GOT TO BREATHE AND EAT AND... ALL *SORTS* OF STUFF.

I WISH IT COULD HAVE GONE ON FOR-EVER. I *WISH* IT DIDN'T HAVE TO END LIKE THAT...

IT ALWAYS ENDS. THAT'S WHAT GIVES IT VALUE.

WHEN YOU GET TO BE ALIVE, EVEN FOR A DAY...

WELL, THERE'S ONLY ONE WAY TO STOP LIVING.

I SUPPOSE SO.

WAS IT WORTH IT?

I ... I DON'T KNOW. I *THINK* SO. I HOPE SO. I MET SUCH NEAT PEOPLE.

AND I HEARD A SONG AND WENT IN TAXI, AND I HAD A H DOG AND A BAGE AND...

SOMEONE HAD ALREADY CALLED 911, BUT THERE WAS NOTHING ANYONE COULD DO. I MEAN, SHE WAS DEAD. TOTALLY DEAD.

AT THE AUTOPSY THING, THE GUY SAID THAT FROM THE CONDITION OF HER LUNGS SHE MUST HAVE BEEN DEAD BY THE TIME SHE HIT THE WATER.

MRS. ROBBINS EXPLAINED SOME OF IT TO ME.

I MEAN, SHE WASN'T *SURPRISED* OR ANYTHING. WHEN I TOLD HER.

I SEE.

DID SHE TELL YOU *ANYTHING* ABOUT HER MEDICAL HISTORY?

DIDI? NO. SHE SAID A LOT OF *OTHER* THINGS, THOUGH.

NO REASON SHE SHOULD HAVE TOLD YOU. NO REASON FOR YOU TO KNOW.

SHE SAID DIDI HAD BEEN SICK SINCE SHE'D BEEN A LITTLE GIRL. THERE WAS SOMETHING WRONG WITH HER HEART.

DIDI HAD NEVER SAID ANYTHING ABOUT IT TO ME.

MRS. ROBBINS SAID THAT SHE'D BEEN LIVING WITH DEATH SINCE SHE WAS SMALL.

MRS. ROBBINS SAID...

YOU KNOW WHAT'S CRAZY, BILLY?

WHAT'S CRAZY IS THAT I ALMOST BE*LIEVED* HER. I ALMOST BELIEVED SHE WAS... WHAT SHE SAID SHE WAS.

BUT THAT *WOULD* BE CRAZY, WOULDN'T IT?

HNN

312

HNNN.

HULLO, DEARIE.

AND *THERE* YOU ARE.

"HOH NO, MAD HETTIE," SHE SAYS, "HI 'AVEN'T SEEN YOUR HEART NOT NOWHERE." "WELL, YOU JUST KEEP LOOKIN'," SAYS I, AND ALL THE TIME SHE'S CARRYIN' IT AROUND WITH HER, BOLD AS A BOLSHEVIK.

AH *SHE'S* A DEEP ONE, AND *THAT'S* NO MISTAKE.

GOODBYE, DEARIO.

STILL, OF ALL THAT LOT, SHE'S THER *ONLY* ONE I'D GIVE *SIXPENCE* FOR.

24

WHAT WERE YOU DOIN' IN *THERE*, THEN, EH? DID I PUT YOU IN THERE? MAYBE I DID. IT'S BEEN A LONG TIME AND ME MIND *DOES* WANDER...

THERE YOU ARE, YOU *PRITTY* THING. ALL THE TROUBLE I'VE BEEN THROUGH TO *FIND* YOU.

NOW, I SUPPOSE I'D BETTER *HIDE* YOU AGAIN.

IF SHE'D STUCK AROUND, I COULD OF ASKED HER ADVICE.

I BET *SHE* COULD OF COME UP WITH SOMEWHERE TO PUT YOU THAT *NO ONE* WOULD THINK OF LOOKIN', NOT IF YOU PAID THEM READY MONEY.

STILL, IT'S NOT AS IF *ANY* OF US ARE GOING ANYWHERE

GIVE HER TIME. *SHE'LL* BE BACK...

☥

the high cost of living

the high cost of living

the high cost of living

on i think of her so much

n fact never. i never just say

i when the sun is on my

ongue and my belly's all warm

n bad days i talk to

eath

IT'S FUNNY BUT ON GOOD DAYS
I DON'T THINK OF HER SO MUCH.
IN FACT NEVER. I NEVER JUST
SAY HI WHEN THE SUN IS ON
MY BACK AND MY BELLY'S ALL
WARM. ON BAD DAYS I TALK TO
DEATH CONSTANTLY NOT ABOUT
NOT DRAMATIC HONESTLY THAT'S

HELLO.

ON THE PAGES INSIDE YOU'LL FIND INFORMATION--PRETTY IMPORTANT INFORMATION--ABOUT... WELL, ABOUT *SEX*, MOSTLY.

NOW, THIS COMIC CONTAINS *WORDS*, *CONCEPTS* AND MAYBE A FEW *IMAGES* THAT SOME PEOPLE *MIGHT* FIND *OFFENSIVE*.

IT'S *PERFECTLY* POSSIBLE THAT YOU MIGHT NOT BE INTERESTED IN THIS. IT'S EVERY BIT AS POSSIBLE THAT YOU SUSPECT YOU'LL BE *OFFENDED* BY ANY MENTION THAT HUMAN BEINGS HAVE THINGS UNDER THEIR CLOTHES, LET ALONE THAT THEY *DO* ANYTHING *INTERESTING* WITH THEM.

IF *YOU* SUSPECT YOU'RE GOING TO BE ONE OF THOSE PEOPLE, THERE'S A REALLY *EASY* SOLUTION TO THIS.

DON'T READ IT. IT'S AS SIMPLE AS THAT.

JUST DON'T READ IT.

AFTER ALL, THE *MOST* IT COULD DO FOR YOU IS TO SAVE YOUR LIFE.

LIFE-- AND I DON'T SUPPOSE I'M THE FIRST TO MAKE THIS COMPARISON -- IS A DISEASE: *SEXUALLY* TRANSMITTED AND INVARI- ABLY *FATAL*.

I SUPPOSE THAT'S *TRUE*, AS FAR AS IT GOES. I MEAN, IF YOU DON'T HAVE *SEX*, YOU DON'T HAVE *LIFE*. BUT ONCE THE LIFE THING STARTS, THERE ARE A NUMBER OF *OTHER* THINGS YOU HAVE TO LOOK OUT FOR.

WHICH IS WHY *I'M* HERE TODAY. THIS IS ABOUT INFORMATION. IF YOU PAY ATTENTION, YOU COULD BE INCREASING YOUR CHANCES OF LIVING A LITTLE LONGER -- FIFTY, SIXTY YEARS MAYBE, IF YOU'RE LUCKY.

NOW, IN THE DISEASE STAKES, SEXUALLY TRANSMITTED DISEASES -- *STD'S* FOR SHORT -- ARE NOTHING MUCH. HEY, YOU CAN CATCH A *COLD* OR 'FLU JUST BY BEING IN A *ROOM* WITH SOMEONE WHO'S GOT IT.

I REMEMBER WHEN SYPHILIS WAS SO PREVALENT THAT HAVING IT BECAME A SORT OF *FASHION* STATEMENT-- PEOPLE WITH SYPHILIS WOULD STICK LITTLE BLACK PATCHES ON THEIR FACES TO HIDE THE MARKS.

PRETTY SOON *EVERYONE* WAS DOING IT.

IF THAT'S IMPORTANT TO YOU, THEN LISTEN UP. OVER THE LAST DECADE ONE DISEASE HAS BEGUN TO SPREAD AND MAKE ITS IMPACT FELT ACROSS THE WORLD. I'M TALKING ABOUT *AIDS* HERE. *AIDS* IS A SEXUALLY TRANS- MITTED DISEASE. IT'S ONE OF A *NUMBER* OF THEM.

MANY OF THEM CAN BE SORTED OUT QUITE QUICKLY WITH ANTIBIOTICS. WHICH IS A GREAT IMPROVEMENT OVER THE WAY THINGS *USED* TO BE. THEY'RE *ALSO* COMPARATIVELY RARE.

ANYWAY. *AIDS* STANDS FOR ACQUIRED IMMUNE DEFICIENCY SYNDROME. IT'S *NOT* A DISEASE THAT KILLS YOU. IT'S A DISEASE THAT DAMAGES YOUR BODY'S IMMUNE SYSTEM AND MAKES IT IN- CREASINGLY DIFFICULT FOR YOUR BODY TO *FIGHT OFF* DISEASE.

AND THE DISEASES YOU *CATCH* KILL YOU.

MOST SCIENTISTS BELIEVE THAT *AIDS* IS CAUSED BY, OR AT LEAST LINKED TO, A VIRUS THEY CALL *HIV* -- HUMAN IMMUNODEFICIENY VIRUS. THE *AIDS* TESTS *DON'T* TEST FOR AIDS, THEY TEST FOR THE PRESENCE OF ANTIBODIES TO *HIV*.

OKAY. LET'S TALK ABOUT HOW YOU *GET* IT. YOU CONTRACT *AIDS* BY EXCHANGING BLOOD OR SEMEN WITH SOMEONE WHO'S GOT IT.

GOT THAT? YOU *CAN'T* GET IT BY SHAKING HANDS, OR BEING IN THE SAME PLACE AS SOMEONE WITH *AIDS*.

YOU COULD EAT OFF THEIR PLATES, WEAR THEIR CLOTHES, *WHATEVER*.

YOU GET IT FROM *INTIMATE CONTACT*.

THE *HIGHEST* RISK ACTIVITIES ARE DIRECT BLOOD TO BLOOD CONTACT -- AS IN, FOR EXAMPLE, USING A SYRINGE NEEDLE SOMEONE ELSE HAS USED BEFORE YOU.

NOW *THAT* ONE'S PRETTY EASILY TAKEN CARE OF: JUST DON'T SHARE NEEDLES. EASY AS THAT. *DON'T*.

IF YOU'RE *STUPID* ENOUGH, OR *DESPERATE* ENOUGH TO USE A NEEDLE SOMEONE ELSE *HAS* USED, THEN YOU'D BETTER WASH THE NEEDLE AND SYRINGE WELL, USING HOUSEHOLD *BLEACH*, AND THEN RINSING WITH WATER; IF YOU'RE IN A STATE OR COUNTRY WHERE THERE'S A LEGAL NEEDLE-EXCHANGE PROGRAM, THEN *USE* IT.

WHERE SEX IS CONCERNED, THE *HIGHEST* RISK ACTIVITY IS UNPROTEC-TED ANAL SEX.

UNPROTECTED VAGINAL SEX IS ALSO *RISKY*.

ORAL SEX IS MUCH *LESS* RISKY, AND *KISSING* IS PRETTY SAFE.

HUGGING IS SAFE AS *HOUSES*. AND WRITING LETTERS IS ABOUT AS RISK-FREE AS YOU CAN *GET*.

LISTEN: YOU *CAN'T* TELL WHO'S GOT AIDS BY *LOOKING* AT THEM. AND *DON'T* KID YOURSELF THAT ONLY CERTAIN *KINDS* OF PEOPLE CAN GET AIDS. THE ONLY PEOPLE WHO CAN GET *AIDS* -- ARE *PEOPLE*.

SKIN COLOR'S NOT IMPORTANT; NEITHER IS WHETHER YOU'RE A MAN OR A WOMAN, WHETHER YOU'RE GAY OR STRAIGHT, SICK OR WELL. AGE DOESN'T MATTER EITHER.

②

AND ONCE YOU'VE *GOT* IT, YOU CAN *SPREAD* IT--THROUGH SEX, OR BY SHARING NEEDLES, OR AS A MOTHER, TO YOUR CHILD BEFORE OR DURING BIRTH.

NOW, THAT *DOESN'T* MEAN THAT YOU SHOULD STOP HAVING SEX ALTOGETHER. BUT MAKE IT *SAFE.* PHRASES LIKE "SAFER SEX" GET BANDIED AROUND A GREAT DEAL. SAFER SEX. WELL, HOW DO YOU PRACTICE SAFER SEX?

FOR A START, IF YOU'RE *HAVING* SEX, YOU SHOULD KNOW WHAT ONE OF *THESE* IS.

IT'S A *CONDOM.* THERE ARE DOZENS OF BRAND NAMES, AND SLANG NAMES FOR THEM. YOU CAN BUY THEM IN DRUG STORES. THEY PREVENT THE PENIS ACTUALLY COMING IN TOUCH WITH THE OTHER PERSON'S BODILY FLUIDS, AND PREVENT SPERM OR BLOOD FROM THE PENIS COMING IN CONTACT WITH THE OTHER PERSON'S BODY.

OKAY. I HAVE A VOLUNTEER HERE WITH ME TO DEMONSTRATE THE *CORRECT* USE OF A CONDOM.

YOU CAN COME *ON* NOW.

HI JOHN.

THIS IS *DEAD* EMBARRASSING.

NONSENSE. BUT THIS DOES BRING ME NEATLY TO MY NEXT POINT. THERE IS A *LOT* OF EMBARRASSMENT CONNECTED WITH POSSESSING, PURCHASING AND USING CONDOMS. BUT WHICH WOULD *YOU* RATHER BE? A LITTLE *EMBARRASSED* OR A LOT *DEAD*?

OKAY, JOHN. LET'S *DO* IT.

I *STILL* THINK THIS IS EMBARRASSING.

FOR DEMONSTRATION PURPOSES, THIS IS A *BANANA*, BY THE WAY. NOT AN ERECT PENIS.

OKAY--TAKE IT *OUT* OF THE PACKET, USING YOUR *FINGERS, NOT* YOUR TEETH. YOU DON'T WANT TO *TEAR* IT.

HOLD IT AT THE *TIP*, SQUEEZING BETWEEN YOUR THUMB AND FOREFINGER, WHILE ROLLING THE CONDOM *DOWN* THE BANANA. UM. *PENIS.*

MAKE SURE THERE'S NO *AIR* TRAPPED IN THE CONDOM, OTHERWISE IT CAN *SPLIT* DURING *SEX*.

YOU WANT *LATEX* CONDOMS, BY THE WAY. OTHER KINDS ARE NO GOOD FOR DISEASE PREVENTION.

OKAY? YOU *GOT* ALL THAT?

THANK YOU, JOHN.

YEAH. ANY TIME.

NOW, SOME PEOPLE DON'T *LIKE* CONDOMS. BUT IF SOMEONE DOESN'T CARE ENOUGH ABOUT YOU TO *WEAR* A CONDOM--OR TO LET *YOU* WEAR A CONDOM--THEY PROBABLY DON'T CARE ENOUGH ABOUT YOU TO BE WORTH HAVING *SEX* WITH. YOU *KNOW?*

④

AFTER USE, DISPOSE OF THE CONDOM SENSIBLY. YOU CAN EAT THE BANANA.

OF COURSE, USING A CONDOM ISN'T THE *ONLY* METHOD OF SAFE SEX. THERE'S NON-PENETRATIVE SEX. THERE'S *OTHER* STUFF YOU CAN DO. *HUGGING, FONDLING, PETTING,* AMONGST OTHER THINGS.

RISK *FREE.*

THERE'S HAVING A MONOGAMOUS RELATIONSHIP WITH SOMEONE WHO'S HAVING A MONOGAMOUS RELATIONSHIP WITH YOU. *AND* ABSTINENCE, OR CHASTITY. IF YOU DON'T *WANT* TO HAVE SEX, THEN *DON'T.* IT'S NOT *THAT* BIG A DEAL.

NOW, A FEW COMMON SENSE THINGS TO BEAR IN MIND. FIRST, ONLY HAVE SEX WITH PEOPLE YOU KNOW WELL. BUT EVEN THAT DOESN'T GUARANTEE *COMPLETE SAFETY*— ONE OF YOU MIGHT ALREADY HAVE THE *HIV* VIRUS.

DON'T HAVE SEX WHILE UNDER THE INFLUENCE OF DRUGS OR ALCOHOL. THAT'S WHEN YOUR RESPONSIBILITY IS AT ITS LOWEST, AND WHEN MOST ACTS OF UN-PLANNED SEX OCCUR. *PLAN AHEAD.*

AIDS ISN'T THE *ONLY* REASON FOR HAVING SAFE SEX. THERE ARE A NUMBER OF OTHERS.

I MENTIONED *STD'S* EARLIER. FEW OF THEM ARE AS *NASTY* AS *AIDS,* BUT *NONE* OF THEM ARE PLEASANT, AND THEY *ALL* HAVE SYMPTOMS AND UNPLEASANT CONSEQUENCES IF LEFT UNTREATED.

GONORRHEA, CHLAMYDIA, HERPES, NON-SPECIFIC URETHRITIS... THERE ARE A WHOLE *BUNCH* OF THEM. WHILE *MOST* OF THEM ARE EASILY TREATED WITH ANTIBIOTICS, SOME OF THEM *CAN'T* BE.

The woman you've just met isn't called Death just because the tuff-sounding name complements her heavy eye makeup and black jeans.

She really *is* Death, the reaper, the one who takes you away when you've had it. It turns out the cloak and the scythe and the skeleton are just bad press; there's nothing grim about her after all.

Discriminating readers have known this since 1989, when she first appeared in her younger brother Dream's monthly comic book, THE SANDMAN. The title had already been making waves as an intelligent, involving adult fantasy series when writer Neil Gaiman and artists Mike Dringenberg and Malcolm Jones III twisted reader expectations by casting dream-weaver Morpheus as the grim, pale, gaunt one and Death as his cheerful foil.

The two are members of the Endless, a loose-knit family of seven who embody their respective realms of Dream, Desire, Despair, Destiny, Delirium, Destruction and Death. Roughly as old as time, they are not merely gods or patron saints; they are the things themselves, personified.

That initial story, "The Sound of Her Wings," first printed in SANDMAN #8, went something like this: feeding pigeons in the park, Dream broods after recovering his domain in the wake of a major setback. His problems had given him a sense of purpose; now that they're largely solved, that sense is gone. Death quotes Mary Poppins — *Death quotes Mary Poppins!* — and draws her brother's feelings out before angrily refusing to indulge his self-pity. Permitting him to tag along as she casually and graciously collects the dead, she cheers him up by sheer example: if she can find satisfaction in her everyday routine, so can he.

Generously displaying her Sunday school sweetness and her rock-club looks over what amounted to 24 pages of sibling interaction (an unusually quiet theme for comics, to say the least), "The Sound of Her Wings" instantly made Death even more popular than the book's title character. Still one of the best-received Sandman stories to date, you can find it in not one but *two* paperback collections: SANDMAN: THE DOLL'S HOUSE and SANDMAN: PRELUDES & NOCTURNES.

Fans demanding to see Death again had to wait a mere four months for SANDMAN #12's "Men of Good Fortune," by Gaiman and artists Michael Zulli and Steve Parkhouse. Here we learned that Death doesn't always take her job completely seriously. Observing tavern life in 14th-century London, she and Dream take special notice of Hob Gadling, a soldier who boasts that his stubborn refusal to die will keep him alive forever. Amused by his impertinence, Death grants him immortality. Over the ensuing centuries, Dream strikes up a fond friendship with this mortal who can't die. Again, Death's light heart enriches what might otherwise be a bleak existence for her brother. "Men of Good Fortune" can be found in the collected SANDMAN: THE DOLL'S HOUSE.

a

brief

history

of

death

Death next appeared in SANDMAN #20, in "Façade," the tragic story of a woman trapped by life, by Gaiman and artists Colleen Doran and Malcolm Jones III. Urania Blackwell wants to kill herself, but a magical artifact of the Egyptian god Ra transformed her into the super-hero Element Girl, and no one can kill Element Girl. When danger threatens, she transmutes into an appropriately defensive element... voluntarily or not. When Death claims her neighbor, Urania begs to be taken, but Death cannot oblige. She does, however, take pity on Element Girl, and helps Urania find her own solution. "Façade" is available in SANDMAN: DREAM COUNTRY.

By now, we've seen Death's devotion to her work, her refusal to take it too seriously, her flippant humor, and, again surprisingly, a hint of a social worker's bleeding heart. Her next appearances, collected in SANDMAN: SEASON OF MISTS, display her willingness to stand against her brother when he is wrong (#21, by Gaiman and Dringenberg) and an unexpectedly flexible approach to her job when circumstances warrant. The latter is apparent in SANDMAN #25, as Gaiman and Jones are accompanied by penciller Matt Wagner. Hell has given up its dead, and a harried, aerobics-outfitted Death has her hands full restoring the proper balance. We see her attempting to collect 13-year-old Charles Rowland and simply giving up when he refuses to come along, preferring to see what life has to offer with his fellow dead boy Edwin Paine.

In SANDMAN SPECIAL #1, by Gaiman and Bryan Talbot, Death exempts another: Dream's son, the Orpheus of myth, who wishes to enter the realm of the dead unscathed to rescue his beloved Eurydice. As an unintended result of her boon, Orpheus survives his own beheading by centuries. This and SANDMAN #31, in which Gaiman and artist Shawn McManus introduce us to Death's favorite king, can be found in SANDMAN: FABLES AND REFLECTIONS.

Nearly every SANDMAN collection contains an appearance by Death, and she continues to appear frequently in his ongoing monthly title (most recently in #53). Her popularity has given her a life beyond Sandman stories, chiefly with the material on view here. The original publication of DEATH: THE HIGH COST OF LIVING helped launch DC's VERTIGO line of comics for mature readers with a remarkable critical and commercial response. "Death Talks About Life" ran as an insert in several pre-VERTIGO titles and met with a tide of interest in its message, causing it to be rereleased later as a public service pamphlet.

The point being: after you've read this book and you find yourself smiling when you think about Death, there's more about her out there.

B I O
G R A
P H I
E S

NEIL GAIMAN *(writer)*

Neil Gaiman is probably best known as the author of the monthly SANDMAN series. His shorter prose work has recently been collected in *Angels & Visitations* (DreamHaven Press). Forthcoming work includes *Mr. Punch* (with Dave McKean) and the BRIEF LIVES Sandman collection.
His house is huge and gothic and a little scary. He mostly writes late at night. He has grandiose plans about answering all his mail but, at present, he probably owes you a letter. If he told you how much he enjoyed working with everyone involved in THE HIGH COST OF LIVING you'd think he was making stuff up again.

CHRISTOPHER BACHALO *(penciller, DEATH: the high cost of living)*

Chris is a native of glamorous Portage La Prairie, Canada, host of the infamous World Curling Championships. Driven to draw after a close encounter of the fifth kind while harvesting wheat, Chris says DEATH: THE HIGH COST OF LIVING was a labor of love. "I had been a longtime fan of SANDMAN and Neil Gaiman, so drawing DEATH was both a pleasure and an honor for me." Eclectic is a good word for this artist's work and personality. His personal likes include Metallica, Rachmaninoff and Neil Diamond, while his work ranges from mystic SHADE, THE CHANGING MAN to Vertigo's CHILDREN'S CRUSADE. When asked to describe his work, Chris simply replied: "Refreshingly different."

MARK BUCKINGHAM *(inker, DEATH: the high cost of living)*

After a brief flirtation with animation followed by a design degree course at Staffordshire University, Mark Buckingham made his comics debut on HELLBLAZER (1988), first as an inker and later as a penciller.
Best known at DC for his inking work on DR. FATE, SHADE, THE CHANGING MAN, THE HACKER FILES, SANDMAN and DEATH: THE HIGH COST OF LIVING, Mark has simultaneously been developing his career as an artist in his own right. As well as joining Neil Gaiman on Miracleman, he has also contributed to SECRET ORIGINS, *Killing Stroke, 2000 AD*, *Ghost Rider* and SWAMP THING.
Mark has co-created *Immortalis* with Nick Vince. Mark's most recent project, *Ghost Rider 2099*, reunites him with his favorite penciller, Chris Bachalo.
Mark and his wife, Gail, currently reside in the seaside town of Clevedon, England.

DAVE MCKEAN *(covers and design, DEATH: the high cost of living; art, DEATH TALKS ABOUT LIFE)*

Dave McKean has illustrated four comics including ARKHAM ASYLUM (DC) and *Signal to Noise* (Gollancz/Dark Horse). He is currently writing and illustrating *Cages (Kitchen Sink)*, a 500-page comic novel about belief, creativity and cats. He has produced all the covers for the ongoing SANDMAN series, is a regular contributor to *The New Yorker* and has done many CD and book covers.
He lives in the Kent countryside with partner Clare and goblin Yolanda.

STEVE OLIFF *(colorist, Death: the high cost of living)*

Steve discovered color theory and Marvel Comics in 1963, color theory by mixing Play-Doh® and being given a full set of Prismacolor pencils (a far cry from crayons). His career was set. Steve has worked for Marvel, Eclipse, Pacific, Byron Preiss Visual Productions, The Dragon, DC, Dark Horse and Image, has colored thousands of pages and has won several comics industry awards. Steve lives in a converted water tower and is the former mayor of Point Arena, California.

TODD KLEIN *(letterer)*

Todd Klein is one of the most versatile and accomplished letterers in comics. He has more than 200 logo designs to his credit, among them THE HECKLER and THE ATLANTIS CHRONICLES for DC. He has also written for comics, including DC's THE OMEGA MEN. Todd is a collector of books, magazines and stamps. He doesn't seem to know why. He also is compelled to keep lists of bird species seen and has been known to travel thousands of miles to see new ones. He and his wife, Ellen, currently reside in rural Southern New Jersey.